It was the night of the full moon.

Groad was digging a big hole. Perched on the edge of the hole, watching him with black beady eyes, was a raven.

Shivers ran up and down Groad's spine. He wanted to run away. But he couldn't.

Suddenly, his shovel hit something hard. It was a chest.

Then Groad heard the sound of wings flapping. He looked up. And there, flying toward him, were the evil ones. The gargoyles.

In the lead was the headless one, its wings outstretched, reaching for him. It was then that he began to scream...

Critters of the Night...
they're here!

MERCER MAYER'S
CRITTERS OF THE NIGHT™

THE HEADLESS GARGOYLE

Written by Erica Farber and J. R. Sansevere

Bullseye Books
Random House ⌂ New York

A BULLSEYE BOOK PUBLISHED BY RANDOM HOUSE, INC.

http://www.randomhouse.com/

Library of Congress Cataloging-in-Publication Data
Farber, Erica.
The headless gargoyle / written by Erica Farber and J. R. Sansevere.
p. cm. — (Mercer Mayer's Critters of the night) "Bullseye books."
SUMMARY: The Howl family races to beat an evil French baron to the head of an
old gargoyle, which will give the owner control over a bunch of stone gargoyles
come to life.
ISBN 0-679-87362-7 (pbk.) [1. Gargoyles—Fiction. 2. Monsters—Fiction.
3. Magic—Fiction.] I. Sansevere, John R. II. Title III. Series: Mayer, Mercer,
1943- Critters of the night.
PZ7.F2275He 1996 [Fic]—dc20 96-21670
RL: 2.7
Printed in the United States of America 10 9 8 7 6 5 4 3 2 1

A BIG TUNA TRADING COMPANY, LLC/J. R. SANSEVERE BOOK

CONTENTS

Wanda

Jack

Thistle

Bones

Snake

Axel

Capt. Short Bob

Dracul Duck

Wolf Mouse

Groad   Frankengator   Moose Mummy

Uncle Mole   Zombie Mombie   Auntie Bell

The Evil Ones

The late Middle Ages…Paris, France…

It was almost midnight. The moon was a round white disk in the black sky. Baron Le Rouge's castle was quiet and dark. Only one light glowed in a tiny room at the top of the castle tower.

A small figure in a dark cape crept silently up the steep stone stairs of the tower. He was the baron's butler, Pierre. Higher and higher he climbed. He was heading for the room at the very top.

Pierre climbed the last step. He tiptoed

quietly up to the door of the tower room. It was ajar. Yellow candlelight flickered across the gray stone walls.

At that moment, a voice began to chant: *"Hax…Pax…Merwin…Malus…"*

The words were not English. And they were not French.

Pierre peered inside. What he saw made him shiver in his very soul.

His master, Baron Le Rouge, was sitting in the shadows. A raven was perched on his shoulder. The baron was reading aloud from a big leather book. And he was mixing up a horrible blue potion inside a skull.

All around the room were skulls and vials of strange herbs and liquids. Skeletons hung from the ceiling. Everything was covered with dust and cobwebs.

The people of the town were afraid of the baron.

They said he was a warlock—the son of an evil witch and a poor mortal.

They claimed he was the master of an army of gray-skinned monsters. The terrible creatures flew through the night to do his evil bidding. Some people believed that once the baron looked at you, you were marked for life.

Pierre took a deep breath. He had to be brave. He had to stop the baron. And he had to do it now, before midnight. Or the powers of darkness would be on the side of his master.

Pierre slowly opened the door and walked inside. He put a silver tray down on the table.

"Pierre, remove that tray at once!" ordered the baron. He glared at Pierre. His eyes gleamed green. They were flecked with black and yellow, like a cat's eyes. "I have no time for food. Soon it will be midnight,

and I must feed my pets the potion of life!
Then they will fly into the darkness and do
as I command!"

The baron threw back his head and
laughed evilly.

Pierre nodded and picked up the tray.
He didn't say anything. He couldn't. His
voice might betray how scared he was.

Scared of what might happen if he failed.

Pierre studied the baron. His face was deathly pale against his red robe. The baron always wore red. In honor of his name—Baron Le Rouge. And of blood, the water of life.

"But it is not food, Master," Pierre finally said. "It is just a goblet of your favorite wine."

Pierre knew his master could not resist his favorite wine. The baron picked up the goblet. He took a big gulp of wine.

"Now, begone!" bellowed the baron. Suddenly, his body slumped backward against his chair.

Pierre smiled. The sleeping potion was working.

"What have you done to me!?" shouted the baron. Then his head fell to the table with a thud. His green eyes were glassy.

The raven uttered a strange, choked cry. His black beady eyes were on Pierre.

Bong…Bong…Bong… The tower bell began to chime the hour. It was midnight.

"You will pay for this, you stupid little toad!" gasped the baron. "I curse you and your descendants. One day the evil ones will come for you. They will destroy your family."

With that, the baron's eyes closed. He was asleep.

The raven flapped his black wings and flew right at Pierre.

Pierre dashed out of the tower room and slammed the door shut behind him. He could hear the raven's angry pecking on the door as he ran down the stairs and out of the castle.

Pierre picked up the heavy mallet he had hidden in the bushes. He fastened it to his belt.

Guided by moonlight, Pierre began to climb up the side of the castle.

At the top of the tower, jutting out

from the stone wall, were the evil ones: the gargoyles. Stone monsters.

The moon cast strange silver shadows across the faces of the gargoyles. In the eerie glow, they looked almost alive. Pierre's eyes widened in fear. His heart began to beat more quickly.

Pierre continued to climb. He had to be brave.

The largest gargoyle was stationed at the top of the tower. He had the body of a dragon, with wings outstretched. His mouth was open, ready to breathe fire. He was the most horrible monster Pierre had ever seen.

He had the kind of evil face you would only see in your worst nightmares.

The monster was the leader of the gargoyles. The baron called him Malus. At midnight when the moon was full, Malus led the others to do the baron's evil bidding.

Pierre climbed up to Malus's evil, leering face. Then, with all his strength, he struck Malus with the mallet. Once. Twice. Three times.

Suddenly, a scream pierced the night. It seemed to come from the tower itself. The head of the gargoyle crashed to the ground below. Then there was silence.

Pierre scrambled down to the ground. He heaved the gargoyle's head into a chest and locked it. He put the key in his pocket.

Then Pierre dragged the chest into the forest and began to dig.

Suddenly, clouds covered the moon. The

forest was plunged into almost total darkness. A strange squawking sound filled the air. Lightning streaked the sky, and it began to rain.

Pierre threw the chest into the hole he had dug. He quickly covered it with dirt.

Rain beat down in torrents. Lightning flashed.

"May the forces of darkness be banished from this land," cried Pierre as he packed down the earth. "And may the power of goodness return."

Pierre's first mission was done. Now he had to get the book. It was filled with magic and enchantments. Dark secrets. He had to get the book before his master awoke.

Pierre ran through the forest to the castle. He looked up at the tower. The stone gargoyles glared evilly down at him. Watching and waiting.

All except for the one called Malus—now the headless gargoyle.

The Magic Book

Present day…Paris, France…

In a small apartment on a narrow, twisting street in Paris, Pierre III lay on his deathbed.

His apartment was on the top floor of a tall building. The old toad's bed was right next to the window.

All day long Pierre stared out the window. His gaze was directed toward the tower of an old stone castle, the Tower of the Headless Gargoyle.

For years, Pierre had watched that tower,

day and night. He was its guardian, always watching and waiting.

Suddenly, a raven landed on Pierre's windowsill. The old toad's eyes widened in fear. He had become very superstitious in his old age. He knew that a raven was a bad omen. It meant something terrible was going to happen.

Pierre tossed in his bed and watched the bird fly away. Then he called for the nurse who sat at his bedside. She got up and stood next to him.

He motioned for her to come closer. She bent low over the bed.

"My time is coming," whispered the old toad. "Get me a pen, a piece of paper, and an envelope."

Pierre put on his reading glasses. He quickly scribbled something on the paper. His handwriting was jagged and hard to read. Then he folded the paper very carefully. He picked up the envelope and addressed it. Then he put the folded piece of paper into the envelope and sealed it.

"Mail this immediately!" the old toad commanded the nurse. "And now bring me the book."

"Which book?" asked the nurse. "You have so many." She pointed to the bookshelves filled with thousands of dusty old leather volumes. Large piles of books also covered the floor. There were books in every room of the apartment.

"The secret book," whispered Pierre to the nurse. He licked his cracked lips as he studied her.

All of a sudden, his mouth had become very dry. The raven flashed through his mind. *A bad omen…*

There is something strange about the nurse, thought Pierre. *What is it?* he wondered.

Aha! She isn't the nurse I usually have at night.

"What happened to Claire?" asked the old toad.

The nurse looked at him and raised her eyebrows in confusion. "Claire who?" she asked.

"Claire, the nurse who has been coming here every night for the last year!" shouted the old toad. He sat up in bed and waved his arms at the nurse.

"Now calm yourself," the nurse said gently. She took his hand in hers and eased him back against the pillows. "You know you're not supposed to get overexcited like that," she soothed. "Your memory is just playing tricks on you. Don't worry. Everything is going to be all right."

"Harrumph," the old toad grunted. But he did as the nurse requested and lay back quietly.

"My name is Marie," said the nurse. "I've been coming to sit with you every night for the past six months."

Pierre took off his glasses and put them on the night table by his bed. He looked over at the nurse, but he didn't know what to say. She was right about his memory. It was going.

Soon he would forget the secrets he had to pass on.

"Which book do you want?" the nurse asked gently.

"The third one in the third row from the top," whispered the old toad. "The one with the red writing on it."

The nurse walked over to the bookcase. She counted the rows of books. Then she stared at the books in the third row.

She reached for a large leather book with iron clasps and blood-red writing on the cover.

The nurse slowly carried the book over to the bed. It was very heavy and hard to hold. Just as she got to the side of the bed, the book suddenly slipped from her hands.

"Oh, no!" she gasped.

The book hit the night table with a thud. It smashed Pierre's glasses.

"Look what you've done!" barked the old toad. "Now I will not be able to read a word!"

"I am so sorry, sir," apologized the nurse. "But the book is very heavy."

"Just mail the letter," grunted Pierre. "And get out of my sight!"

The nurse rushed from the room. She closed the door behind her.

Pierre clutched the book in his arms. At least the book was safe.

But the raven…A bad omen…

The old toad fell into a deep, troubled sleep.

Sometime later, the bedroom door slowly

creaked open. The hall light cast a thin beam of light into the darkened room. It was just enough to reveal the sleeping silhouette of Pierre. And the rows of books.

The nurse crept into the room. She tip-toed over to the bookcase. She reached for the third book on the third shelf. Then she slipped quietly out of the room.

The old toad stirred in his bed. He turned over. His eyes opened just as the door closed.

Has someone been in the room? he wondered. *It couldn't have been the nurse. I sent her home.* His mind was playing tricks on him again.

Pierre slowly eased his body out of bed and into his wheelchair. He needed a drink of water.

He wheeled himself out of his room and down the hall. The envelope he had given the nurse was lying on the table.

At that moment, there was a loud knock on the closet door. *Rap, rap. Rap, rap.*

What can that be? the old toad wondered. It sounded much too loud to be a mouse or a rat. He threw open the closet door. There was Claire, the night nurse, bound and gagged.

The old toad quickly untied Claire's bonds. She gasped for breath. "A man in a red cloak with horrible green eyes tied me up and put me in here," she gasped.

Pierre frowned, deep in thought. Green eyes. Now he knew what had been so strange about that nurse. It was her eyes. They were green flecked with black and yellow, like a cat's eyes. And they could belong only

to one person… Baron
Le Rouge III.

"The magic book!"
shouted Pierre as he
wheeled himself back
into his bedroom.
Claire followed him.

He picked up the heavy leather book
that was by his bed. "What does this say?"
asked the old toad frantically.

Claire peered at the dusty red writing.
"'*Secret Family Recipes,*'" she said.

"Oh, no!" gasped Pierre. "Check the
shelf! Third row, third book, the one with
the red writing. Get it!"

Claire walked over to the bookcase.
Slowly, she turned around. "It's gone," she
said.

The old toad slumped down in his wheelchair. The baron had the book—the book he
had guarded every day of his life. The book
that held the secrets of darkness…

Groad's Nightmare

Far across the sea, it was a dark and moon-less night in Critter Falls. At Old Howl Hall, Groad, the Howls' cook and butler, was lying in bed. He slept deeply.

Groad moaned softly in his sleep. He was having a nightmare…

…It was the night of the full moon. He was digging a big hole. Perched on the edge of the hole, watching him with black beady eyes, was a raven.

The raven uttered a strange, choked cry. Shivers ran up and down Groad's spine. He wanted to run away. But he couldn't.

He had to keep digging.

Suddenly, his shovel hit something hard. It was a chest. The chest gleamed in the moonlight.

Then Groad heard the sound of wings flapping. He looked up. And there, flying toward him, were the evil ones. The gargoyles. He gasped and dropped the shovel.

In the lead was the headless one, its wings outstretched, reaching for him. It was then that he began to scream…

Groad bolted out of bed. He stared around his room in a panic. "Eet was just a nightmare," he murmured to himself.

It was the same nightmare he had had ever since he was a boy. In the nightmare, he was always digging. There was always a full moon. And they always came for him just when he had found the chest.

The gargoyles were always led by the headless one.

Groad shivered. He looked out his bedroom window. It gave him a perfect view of the swamp and the cemetery at Old Howl Hall.

The sky was gray and rainy. It was the kind of horrible weather Groad loved most.

Suddenly, his bedroom door flew open. Axel and Thistle Howl ran inside and jumped on the bed. It was a special bed made of nails. It worked wonders for Groad's back.

"Groad, are you okay?" asked Axel.

"You were screaming," added Thistle.

"I am fine," answered Groad. "I was just...um...doing my morning stretches. Screaming ees part of ze exercise."

"We're hungry," said Axel. "What's for breakfast?"

"'Ow about Brains Benedict and Beetle Juice?" suggested Groad.

"Yummy," said Thistle.

Axel and Thistle followed Groad downstairs. Kitty, the Howls' pet saber-toothed tiger, was sleeping by the front door. As soon as she saw Groad, she stood up and roared.

"I guess Kitty's hungry, too," said Axel.

Groad patted Kitty on the head.

"Nice kitty," Groad said. "'Ow about some of zat left-over monkey meat? Eet ees still very bloody, just ze way you like eet."

Kitty wagged her tail.

Suddenly, the doorbell rang.

"Who could zat be at zees early 'our?" grumbled Groad.

Axel opened the door.

"Special delivery," said the mailman.

Kitty walked over to the door. She loved visitors. She opened her mouth wide and growled at the mailman.

The mailman took one look at Kitty and dropped the envelope he was holding. Then he took off down the driveway.

"Wonder what he was in such a big hurry about," said Thistle.

Axel picked up the envelope. Groad's name was written on it in scrawling, jagged letters.

"It's for you," said Axel. He handed Groad the envelope.

Groad studied the envelope. There was a Paris postmark on it. His heart began to race. A shiver ran down his spine. He didn't know why.

With shaking hands, he tore open the letter.

Just then, Jack and Wanda Howl came down the stairs.

"What is it, Groad?" asked Wanda.

Groad read the letter out loud:

Groad— YOU MUST come at ONCE. It is a Matter of life and death. Of good versus evil. The time has come for you to lead the battle. You must banish the powers of darkness from the land. It is YOUR DESTINY!

—Your great Uncle Pierre III

The Gargoyles Awake

Deep in the woods outside Paris was a small cottage. It was nestled among the tall old trees.

No one dared enter the woods. People told stories about strange flashing lights and large beasts crashing through the trees. Everyone agreed that the woods were haunted.

That night, as the moon rose high in the sky, a raven flew into the cottage window. It squawked loudly at its master...Baron Le Rouge III.

The baron turned to the raven. His lips curled into a cold, hard smile. His green eyes gleamed. He picked up the heavy leather book from the scarred wooden table. He put a vial of strange, glowing blue liquid in the pocket of his red cloak.

"Come, raven," he called. "The hour is almost upon us. We must feed our pets the potion of life!"

The raven squawked once again. Then it perched on its master's shoulder. Baron Le Rouge closed the cottage door and strode through the deserted woods.

An owl hooted in a tree. Branches creaked in the wind. The moon shone silver in the blackened sky.

Baron Le Rouge had waited his entire life for this moment. He was the last of his family. A dying breed.

He had to do it—for the sake of his ancestors.

He had to keep the name Le Rouge alive.

He had to reclaim the castle…and the evil ones. The gargoyles.

Baron Le Rouge leaned back and laughed into the cold, starry sky. His laughter rang out harshly in the quiet woods.

He couldn't have asked for a better night. It was a perfect night to reawaken the evil ones.

Baron Le Rouge hurried to the Tower of the Headless Gargoyle. It was almost midnight.

The baron stared up at the stone monsters.

They shone silver in the moonlight. Their faces were streaked with strange shadows.

The raven squawked once and then flew into the castle.

Baron Le Rouge followed. Slowly, he climbed the old stone steps to the tower.

The baron breathed loudly. The steps were very steep. The secret magic book was heavy in his hands. But still the raven flew upward.

Finally, they reached the tower room at the top of the stairs.

Baron Le Rouge threw open the massive wooden door. Pale silver moonlight flooded the room.

The baron crossed the room. He looked out the window. There they were. The evil ones. The gargoyles.

Just then, the tower bell rang twelve times. It was midnight.

The baron clambered out the window. He stood on a narrow stone ledge. His red cape billowed around him in the wind.

Then he opened the magic book. He sprinkled the strange blue liquid onto the stone gargoyles.

And then he chanted, *"Hax…Pax… Merwin…Malus…"*

Suddenly, the gargoyle statues began to shudder. And to shake. Something shrieked in the night.

One by one, the gargoyles came to life. They flew off the tower and into the darkness.

Baron Le Rouge smiled an evil smile. The raven screeched and settled on his shoulder. Then the baron made his way back into the tower room and down the stairs.

Outside, the baron stared at the gargoyles. They had gathered at the fountain in the center of the castle courtyard. They were dipping their wings in the water.

"Go, gargoyles!" commanded Baron Le Rouge. "Go into the night and make some mischief. Bring back gold and jewels. Now you belong to me."

But the gargoyles didn't move. They stayed in the fountain.

"Go, gargoyles!" screamed Baron Le Rouge. "Go *now!*"

But still the gargoyles would not listen.

The baron's pale face reddened with anger. He glared at the gargoyles.

Suddenly, he heard a loud crash. The earth rumbled beneath his feet.

The gargoyles froze. They stared at the creature standing behind the baron.

The baron turned around.

Before him was the enormous body of the headless gargoyle.

The gargoyle took another step and then crashed into a tree. It fell to the ground with an earth-shaking thud.

The raven uttered his strange, choked cry and flew in circles around the empty space where the gargoyle's head should have been.

"The head!" Baron Le Rouge suddenly

screamed. "He is their leader, and he cannot lead them without his head! I must find the gargoyle's missing head!"

Baron Le Rouge knew just what he had to do.

The Crypt of Passion

The next morning, far below the streets of Paris, Groad and the Howls lay sleeping. They were in a circular stone room deep in the catacombs. It was called the Crypt of Passion.

The crypt was dark and creepy. Rats scuttled in and out of the crumbling stone walls. In the center of the room was a huge pile of bones. The bones dated back to the French Revolution.

The whole place smelled damp and musty.

Like the home of the dead.

Wanda Howl yawned and stretched. She nudged her husband, Jack, with her elbow. "I'm so glad we decided to come to Paris with Groad," said Wanda. "Isn't it romantic, darling?" She gazed happily around the crypt.

"Quite so," agreed Jack. "The place hasn't changed much since our honeymoon. Although it looks as if there may be more bones on the pile."

Axel sat up and stared at his parents. "It must have taken a million skeletons to make that pile of bones," he said.

"I wonder how all those people died," said Thistle. "Do you think they were tortured?" She grinned at the thought.

"It's marvelous for the children to be surrounded by so much history," commented Jack. "We must take them to the torture chambers before we leave."

"Yes," agreed Wanda. "But, remember, this morning you and I are supposed to go to the guillotine."

"It will be just like it was on our honeymoon," said Jack with a smile. "Only there won't be a beheading. I don't think they chop off people's heads much anymore."

"You two enjoy your second 'oneymoon," said Groad. "Ze children can come with me to see my great-uncle. After all, zat ees why I am 'ere."

"That's a wonderful idea!" exclaimed Wanda. "We'll see you tonight."

"It is the night of the full moon, you know," said Jack with a gleam in his eyes.

Groad, Axel, and Thistle took the subway to the last stop. They were all the way on the other side of town.

It was a bright, sunny day. The sun glinted on the river. Groad looked around at the buildings. He smelled the damp river air and smiled.

It reminded him of his childhood.

Just then, Groad heard a strange, choked cry. He looked up. There, circling the entrance to his great-uncle's building, was a raven.

The raven's eyes were black and beady. Death's eyes.

Groad shivered in the warm sunlight. A big black raven. It was just like the raven in his nightmare.

"Are we there yet?" asked Thistle, tugging on his sleeve.

Groad shook his head. He didn't know why he kept thinking about his nightmare. It was only a dream, after all. Nothing to worry about.

"'Ere we are," announced Groad finally as he, Axel, and Thistle came to an old stone building. It was the tallest building on the block.

A man opened the door. He was dressed in a blue suit with gold buttons. He was wearing a matching blue hat with gold trim. He held the door for them with a white-gloved hand.

"*Bonjour,*" said the doorman.

"*Bonjour,*" said Groad, walking into the

lobby. "Zat means good day," he said to Axel and Thistle.

Their footsteps echoed on the lobby's marble floor. They stopped in front of an old-fashioned wrought-iron elevator. The doorman followed them. He pulled the door shut with a bang.

"What floor?" asked the doorman.

"Ninth, please," replied Groad.

The doorman pushed down a red lever. With a lurch, the elevator rose. It hummed loudly as it began to climb the floors.

"As I told you before," Groad said to Axel and Thistle, "my great-uncle ees a leetle cookoo. 'E likes to talk about ze powers of darkness. And when 'e really gets going, 'e starts in on ze gargoyles."

"What gargoyles?" asked Axel.

Groad just shrugged. "I don't know," he said.

"Ninth floor," the door-man announced.

He pulled open the elevator door. Groad and Thistle got out right away.

But just at that moment, the doorman dropped all of his change. Coins fell out of his pocket and all over the floor of the elevator. Axel bent down to help him pick up the money.

The doorman shut the door before Axel could get out. Axel looked up in surprise.

The doorman was staring down at him. He had the strangest green eyes, flecked with black and yellow. Axel had never seen eyes like that before.

They were the last things Axel saw before he was plunged into total darkness.

Leader
of the Pack

Groad and Thistle walked down the hall-way. They didn't notice that Axel was no longer behind them.

Groad knocked on the door of his great-uncle's apartment. There was no answer.

He knocked again.

"Maybe he's not home," said Thistle.

Groad frowned. He was just about to knock again when he heard a sound from behind the apartment door.

Creak, creak.

The door slowly cracked open an inch.

The chain was still drawn.

"Who is it?" rasped a gravelly voice.

"Eet ees Groad, your great-nephew," Groad announced.

"How do I know it is really you?" the gravelly voice asked.

Groad looked down at Thistle. She rolled her eyes.

"You sent me a letter, remember?" said Groad. "You said eet was a matter of life and death. Zat eet was my destiny." Groad sighed. It sounded so silly.

Slowly, the chain was removed and the door opened.

Thistle turned to look at Axel. He wasn't there. She wondered where he could have gone. She was just about to tell Groad that Axel was missing when she spotted him running down the hall toward her.

"Hurry up!" called Thistle.

Axel followed Thistle and Groad into the apartment.

Pierre III, Groad's great-uncle, was sitting in a wheelchair. He had a plaid rug over his knees.

"Who are they?" asked the old toad suspiciously. He glared at Axel and Thistle.

"This is Thistle Howl," said Groad. "And this is Axel."

Pierre studied the children for a long moment. Axel looked down at the ground. The old toad's gaze was making him uncomfortable.

"You look very familiar to me," Pierre murmured, staring at Axel. "I feel as if I've met you somewhere before."

Thistle, Axel, and Groad followed the old toad down the hall into his bedroom.

"Listen to me carefully," Pierre said to Groad. "There is not much time left."

Groad frowned. His great-uncle was even more "cookoo" than he remembered.

"Tonight is the third and final night of the full moon," said the old toad. "And Baron Le Rouge will animate the gargoyles once again. He has the magic book!"

"What are you talking about?" asked Groad.

"First the baron needs the head," Pierre continued gravely, ignoring Groad.

"Whose head?" asked Groad.

"The head of Malus, the leader of the gargoyles," explained the old toad. "Malus lost his power long ago when your great-great-great-uncle Pierre chopped off his head. That is why the tower is known as the

Tower of the Headless Gargoyle."

Pierre pointed out the window toward the castle.

"Baron Le Rouge III stole an ancient magic book from me. It holds the secrets of darkness," he continued. "And now that he has it, he can bring the tower's stone gargoyles to life. But it can only be done at midnight when the moon is full. We must not let the baron find Malus's head. If Malus stares into Baron Le Rouge's eyes, he will fall under the baron's evil power. The world will no longer be safe from the powers of darkness."

"Well, where ees zis 'ead?" asked Groad. "Ees zere a map?"

"The map is in here," said Pierre. He pointed to his head with a long, bony finger. "And after I tell you, *you* will be responsible for keeping Malus's head out of Le Rouge's hands!"

"Me?" gasped Groad.

"Yes," snapped Pierre impatiently. "It is your destiny. Do I have to keep reminding you? The head is buried in a chest in the woods by the castle. Follow the tower's shadow in the moonlight. The tip of the shadow will meet the fountain. Then go north twenty paces. And east thirty paces. That is where the head is buried."

"Excuse me," said Axel suddenly. "I've got to go to the bathroom."

"It's down the hall, second door on the right," said Pierre.

Axel walked quickly out of the room. Seconds later, they heard the sound of glass

breaking. It came from the bathroom.

Groad charged down the hallway. Thistle and Pierre were right behind him. Groad turned the doorknob. The door was locked.

"Axel, are you in zere?" shouted Groad.

There was no answer.

"Stand back," commanded Groad. "We must break ze door down."

Groad hurled his body against the door. With a crash, it burst open.

A black raven was sitting on the window sill. There was glass all over the floor. Axel was gone.

"It was the baron!" shouted Pierre. "He must have gone out the window."

The raven uttered a strange, choked cry. Then it flew out the window and disappeared.

Thistle and Groad stared at the old toad.

"That boy was not really Axel," Pierre explained. "It was Baron Le Rouge in the form of Axel."

"What do you mean?" asked Groad, trying to keep the panic out of his voice.

"The baron has the power to transform himself into other shapes," explained the old toad.

"So where's the real Axel?" asked Thistle.

"We've got to find 'im," said Groad, moving out of the room.

"Listen to me," ordered the old toad harshly. "We must move the gargoyle's head tonight. Before the baron finds it. We will do it under the cover of darkness, after the full moon rises... before midnight. Just remember, if the clock strikes twelve before our work is done, all will be lost."

Groad's nightmare flashed through his mind again. It always began with a raven, and it always ended with a head... a gargoyle's head.

So it was not just a dream after all. It *was* his destiny!

Groad dashed out of Pierre's apartment to find Axel. He pressed the elevator button. Thistle and Pierre were right behind him. They watched as the arrow slowly climbed to the ninth floor.

As soon as the elevator came to a stop, Groad yanked open the door. Lying on the floor was a lumpy burlap sack. The sack was wiggling.

"Help!" came a muffled cry from inside the sack.

Quickly, Groad untied the rope that held the sack closed. Out came Axel. He rubbed his eyes.

"What happened?" asked Axel.

"Sank goodness you are safe," said Groad in relief. He hugged Axel tightly.

Axel looked at him in surprise. "You know what, Groad?" he said. "You're getting mushy in your old age."

Thistle and Groad just laughed.

"To the basement!" Pierre commanded. He wheeled himself into the elevator. "We must get the picks and shovels. Malus's head was buried in a chest. The key is in my pocket."

He pulled an old gold key out of his pocket. It glinted dully in the hallway light.

"After that, we must go to the castle and wait for the moon to rise."

Midnight

The night was cold and clear. The wind whistled through the cracks in the old stones of the castle. Stars shone in the sky as the moon rose slowly, a round yellow ball suspended between the trees.

Axel, Thistle, Groad, and Pierre were hiding in the shadows of the castle courtyard. The tower stood tall and dark before them.

"Hurry, moon!" said Thistle. She shifted impatiently as she stared at the sky.

"Silence, child!" commanded Pierre from his wheelchair. "We do not want the baron to know we are here."

"But he's not here," said Axel, glancing around the empty courtyard.

The whites of the old toad's eyes glinted in the darkness. "Just because you cannot see him does not mean he is not here," said Pierre softly.

Groad stared at the moon. It was almost above the tower now. It had lost its yellow cast and had turned a silvery white color. Pierre was looking at the moon too.

"It is time," he whispered to Groad.

Groad grabbed the pick and shovels. Thistle carried the bucket. Axel pushed the old toad in his wheelchair as they made their way across the courtyard.

"Hurry!" urged Pierre. "It is after eleven. We have less than an hour to dig up the chest and get the gargoyle's head."

Groad and Thistle both ran toward the fountain.

"I can see the shadow!" called Thistle excitedly.

Axel ran after them. He pushed the old toad's wheelchair faster and faster.

Suddenly, the wheel-chair hit a big rock and flew up in the air. Pierre began to fall.

Axel yanked the chair back as hard as he could. Pierre sat up. "Be careful!" he warned Axel.

Axel nodded as he continued toward Groad and Thistle.

"…seventeen…eighteen…nineteen… twenty…" murmured Groad, walking north.

"Now thirty paces east," said Thistle.

"One…two…three…" began Groad, turning to his right and walking east.

It was then that they heard an eerie, choking cry. It seemed to fill the entire courtyard. Groad paused and looked over at Pierre.

"Keep walking!" ordered the old toad. "Do not stop!"

Axel and Thistle looked at each other. Their eyes were round with excitement… and fear.

"…twenty-seven…twenty-eight… twenty-nine…thirty…" said Groad. Then he began to dig. The earth was cold and hard. It was filled with rocks and stones. He had to use the pick to hack through the stones. It was hard work.

Soon his shoulders were sore. His hands

were blistered. And his body was wet with perspiration. But still he kept digging.

The hole became deeper and deeper. The earth rose around Groad like a grave.

Axel and Thistle yanked out each bucket of earth and dumped it. The old toad held the flashlight, illuminating the hole. His hands shook, making the light bounce around the hole. It created weird shadows.

"Dig faster!" shouted Pierre. "Soon it will be midnight."

The old toad looked up at the tower. He could see the dark shapes of the gargoyles outlined in the moonlight. Something was moving in the tower window. He knew it had to be the baron, waiting for the clock to strike twelve.

Axel and Thistle checked Pierre's watch. "It's almost midnight," Axel said.

"There's only five minutes left," added Thistle in a worried voice.

Suddenly, Groad's shovel hit something hard. He fell to his knees. With his hands he pushed the dirt away. It was a chest.

The chest gleamed in the moonlight… just as in his dream.

"I found ze chest!" shouted Groad. "Give

me ze key. 'Urry! Eet ees almost midnight."

Pierre reached into his pocket. He felt for the cold, hard lump that should have been there, but it was gone. "Oh, no!" he gasped. "I must have dropped the key when I almost fell by the fountain."

The old toad began to wheel himself wildly toward the fountain.

Suddenly, the clock began to toll.

Bong…Bong…Bong…Bong…

Groad looked up in a panic. "Where is my great-uncle?" he asked.

"He's looking for the key," said Thistle.

"Break the lock with your shovel!" Axel yelled down to Groad. "It's the only way!"

Bong…Bong…Bong…Bong…

With all his might Groad pounded the shovel against the old metal lock. At last, it popped off with a cracking sound.

Groad grunted as he lifted the heavy lid of the chest.

Inside it was the gargoyle's head.

Bong…Bong…Bong…

Groad lifted the head and put it on the ground next to the chest.

Bong… It was twelve o'clock…midnight.

A terrible screeching sound came from the tower. Seconds later, the pack of gargoyles flew off the tower and into the night.

"Hurry, Groad!" shouted Axel.

Suddenly, Malus's eyes opened. They glowed in the moonlight.

Groad froze. He was mesmerized by the glowing eyes of the gargoyle's head.

"Pierre?" grunted Malus.

Shivers ran up and down Groad's spine. This couldn't be real. It had to be a dream.

Groad willed himself to wake up. But he already knew deep down inside that he couldn't wake up. He was already awake.

It wasn't a dream. It was real.

Groad took a deep breath. He had to be brave. He looked into the strange, glowing eyes of Malus.

"No, I am not Pierre," Groad said to the head. "I am 'is great-great-great-nephew, Groad. You must leesten to me. Baron Le Rouge ees coming for you. If you look into 'is eyes, you will be forever in 'is power. 'E will send you out into ze night to do evil. Darkness will descend on ze land."

Groad stopped and licked his lips. The words seemed to have come out of nowhere.

Suddenly, he heard the sound of wings flapping. The raven circled the hole.

"Hurry, the gargoyles are coming!" barked Pierre as he neared Groad. "Give me the head!"

Groad lifted the head up toward the old toad. "Remember," Groad said to Malus. "No matter what 'appens, do not look into ze baron's eyes. For zen all will be lost."

The old toad grabbed the gargoyle's head and put it on his lap. He wheeled himself away from the hole. Groad clambered out.

What he saw chilled him to his very bones. They were surrounded by gargoyles. One was holding Axel. Another was holding Thistle.

Groad's eyes sought Pierre's. But they were not the eyes Groad remembered. They were cat's eyes, green flecked with black and yellow.

Suddenly, a cloud of smoke engulfed Pierre. When the smoke cleared, he was gone. Baron Le Rouge III stood in his place. He held the magic book and Malus's head high in the air and laughed. "Come, my pet!" the baron commanded. "Come for your head!"

The earth rumbled beneath their feet. Trees crashed to the ground as the headless gargoyle came lumbering toward the baron, his wings outstretched, reaching for his head.

The Gargoyle's Head

"Let ze children go!" commanded Groad. He stared boldly into Baron Le Rouge's cold green eyes. "Zey have nothing to do with zis. You may do what you wish with me, but let zem go!"

The raven circled above Groad.

The baron did not reply. He just pointed at Groad. Two gargoyles came forth from the circle and grabbed him.

Baron Le Rouge turned to the huge body of the headless gargoyle. "Come for your head!" he thundered.

The headless gargoyle lumbered forward.
"Kneel!" commanded the baron.

Malus covered the ground between them in one step. Then he knelt before the baron. No one moved. All eyes were on Baron Le Rouge as he placed Malus's head on top of his body.

The leader of the gargoyles stood up. He flapped his wings and let out a roar that shook the tower itself. Stones tumbled to the ground.

"Take them to the tower!" shouted the baron. He pointed to Groad, Axel, and Thistle. "We will deal with them there. Pierre is already there. We will push them off the top of the tower. Their skulls will crack open on the stones of the courtyard. They will die instantly."

The baron laughed coldly. The raven uttered his strange, choked cry.

"You will never get away with zis!" screamed Groad, his eyes wild with fear and fury. "Never!"

"Of course I will, you stupid little butler!" said Baron Le Rouge. "It will look like an unfortunate accident."

There is only one hope left: Malus! thought Groad. *If only Malus doesn't look into the baron's eyes, there is a chance that he could save us.*

But before Groad could say or do anything, Malus grabbed him between his claws. Then he flapped his wings and took off, with Groad in his clutches.

The other gargoyles flew with the baron toward the tower.

The moonlight shone more brightly on the top of the tower. It lit up the gruesome faces of the gargoyles like a spotlight.

Just as Baron Le Rouge had said, Pierre was already there. A gargoyle had pushed his wheelchair to the ledge surrounding the tower.

One little push and the old toad would fall to his doom.

The Raven

"To the ledge!" commanded Baron Le Rouge.

The gargoyles pushed Axel and Thistle over to the ledge, next to Pierre. Malus stood behind the old toad, holding Groad.

Groad looked over the ledge. The courtyard lay far below, shrouded in darkness.

Axel and Thistle had stopped struggling. They were no match for the gargoyles.

"Throw Groad first!" Baron Le Rouge commanded Malus.

Groad tried to look into Malus's glowing

eyes. But it was too late. Malus was under the power of the baron. Groad tried to swallow the lump of fear in his throat. He had to think of something.

Suddenly, Malus looked at Groad. Their gazes met and held. Something passed between them in that split second. Something powerful.

Malus turned sharply. He opened his mouth and roared in the baron's face. Icy fire spewed forth from Malus's gaping jaws. Before their eyes, the baron was transformed one final time.

He was now a stone gargoyle statue: the most horrible of them all. Clasped in his claws was the magic book. It had also turned to stone.

"Release them!" Malus commanded the other gargoyles.

Axel and Thistle ran to Groad. Groad put an arm around each of them.

Slowly, the stones of the tower began to turn pink in the glow of the rising sun.

Malus gathered his wings and resumed his position in the center of the tower. The other gargoyles followed. All except for the baron. He would remain on the tower ledge forever.

"Your great-great-great-uncle Pierre would be proud of you," Malus told Groad.

Then his eyes closed, and he turned back into stone.

Just then Jack and Wanda scrambled onto the tower roof.

"Oh, you must be Groad's great-uncle," said Wanda to the old toad. "So nice to meet you. What a beautiful view." She looked over the edge of the tower at the gargoyles. "And those statues are breathtaking. A marvelous place for you to have brought the children, Groad. I'm sure it's a memory of Paris they'll never forget."

Groad, Axel, and Thistle exchanged glances.

Jack held up the gold key. "We found this key by the fountain," he said.

"We no longer need that key," said Pierre. He got up out of his wheelchair and stood before them.

Groad, Axel, and Thistle gasped.

"You can walk!" exclaimed Thistle.

"You're all right!" said Axel.

"But I thought…" began Groad.

"I'm fine," said the old toad. "All of a sudden, my strength has returned."

Pierre looked at Groad and smiled. "Destiny is a powerful thing. It works in mysterious ways. When its call is answered, just about anything can happen."

Suddenly, a strange, choked cry filled the air. A black raven swooped down from the sky and circled the tower.

"Oh, a raven," said Jack, looking up at the bird. "Some say a raven is an omen."

Axel, Thistle, Groad, and Pierre looked at one another. Nobody said a word.

Then the raven flew away from the tower and disappeared from sight.